Treasure Hunt

Twink

Bimi

Pix

Sooze

Sili

Mariella

Kiki

Ivy

Book Ten

Treasure Hunt

Titania Woods

Illustrated by Smiljana Coh

LONDON BERLIN NEW YORK

Bloomsbury Publishing, London, Berlin and New York

First published in Great Britain in 2009 by Bloomsbury Publishing Plc
36 Soho Square, London, W1D 3QY

A CIP catalogue record of this book is available from the British Library

ISBN 978 0 7475 9832 9

All papers used by Bloomsbury Publishing are natural, recyclable products made
from wood grown in well-managed forests. The manufacturing processes conform to
the environmental regulations of the country of origin.

Typeset by Dorchester Typesetting Group Ltd
Printed in Singapore by Tien Wah Press

1 3 5 7 9 10 8 6 4 2

www.glitterwingsacademy.co.uk

To my husband,
the treasure of my life

Chapter One

The sun shone brightly as Twink Flutterby skimmed over summer-green fields with her mother and sister. On such a lovely morning, the journey to Glitterwings Academy should have been the most delightful thing in the world.

Twink hardly noticed it. She cast furtive glances at her mother as they flew. Although Mrs Flutterby was clearly trying to act as if nothing was wrong, she seemed tired and worried. Twink bit her lip, wondering whether she should mention what she had overheard the night before.

Fortunately, Teena was too excited about returning to school to pick up on the mood. 'Oh, I can hardly wait!' she cried, doing a quick somersault in the air. 'Are we almost there, Mum?'

'Almost,' said Twink's mother. 'It's just over this hill.'

'Hurrah!' Teena darted ahead, her wings a lavender blur. A moment later she was back again. 'Mum, I can see Zuzu! I'm going to go and say hello, all right?' Without waiting for an answer, Twink's little sister sped off to greet her best friend.

In the sudden silence, Twink's mother gave her a keen look. 'You're very quiet today. Is something wrong?'

Twink looked down at her oak-leaf bag, playing with its clasp. 'No, I'm fine,' she said.

Her mother touched her arm, bringing them both to a halt. 'Are you sure?' Her violet eyes were gentle and worried.

Twink could hold it in no longer. 'Oh, Mum, I – I heard you and Dad talking about Gran last night, and how you have to go to her straight away. What's wrong? Is she all right?' Her words tumbled over each other.

Her mother winced. 'Oh, Twink . . . we were hoping that we wouldn't have to worry you. I – well, I'm afraid your gran isn't very well.'

'What's wrong with her?' asked Twink. Her wings felt cold, despite the warmth of the summer day.

'Come, let's sit down,' said her mother, gliding towards the ground. When they were both settled on a smooth round stone, she put her arm around Twink. 'You know that your gran caught that wing-chill last month,' she said.

Twink leaned against her mother's side. 'Yes, but – but you and Dad said it wasn't serious,' she mumbled.

'It wasn't,' said her mother. 'And she's mostly over it now, but she's not really perking up the way she should. The doctor says that she's gone into the Doldrums.'

The word sent a shiver up Twink's spine. 'What's that?' she whispered.

'It's – well, it's when a fairy feels a bit down,' said Twink's mother. 'She needs cheering up, you see. So your father and I are going to go and visit her, and do what we can.'

'Will she be all right?' Twink gazed anxiously into her mother's eyes.

Her mother hesitated, and then gave a firm nod. 'Yes, I'm sure she will be. We just have to think positive.'

Twink's heart seemed to miss a beat. What did *that* mean? Was her gran going to be all right or not?

'But Twink, please don't tell Teena,' added her mother. 'I don't want to worry her.' She smiled ruefully, smoothing Twink's long pink hair. 'I didn't want to worry *you* either, but maybe it's better that you know. I keep forgetting how grown-up you are now.'

In spite of everything, Twink felt a rush of pride that her mother thought she was growing up.

'Don't worry, I won't tell Teena,' she said. 'But Mum . . .' she paused, uncertain how to put her fears into words. She just knew she'd feel a lot less worried if her mother didn't seem so concerned.

Her mother squeezed her arm as if she understood. 'Gran will be fine, darling; I promise. Now, let's fly on to school before Teena starts to wonder where we've got to!'

As Twink and her mother crested the grassy hill, Glitterwings Academy came into view: a large, spreading oak tree rising up from a field of flowers. Tiny arched windows wound their way up the tree trunk, and the grand double doors at its base stood open in welcome.

While her mother went off to find Teena, Twink flew slowly to the third-year area, thinking of Gran. The Doldrums sounded so scary! Would her grandmother really be all right?

'Welcome back!' said Miss Twilight, ticking Twink off on her clover-leaf list. She was a tall, dramatic-looking fairy with bright silver hair and purply-grey wings. 'Looking forward to the new term?'

'I suppose,' said Twink. Miss Twilight gave her a considering look. 'I mean, yes!' Twink went on

hastily. 'I just love the summer term. Glitterwings is so pretty then!'

Oh great – I sound like Mum! she thought. Twink's mother used to be a student at Glitterwings herself, and was always exclaiming over its beauty in every season.

To Twink's relief, Miss Twilight agreed. 'Yes, it *is* pretty now, isn't it? And I've got a special surprise for the Third Years this term, too!'

'What, Miss Twilight?' asked Twink, interested despite herself.

Her year head laughed. 'Now, it wouldn't be a surprise if I told you, would it?' The tiny moonstones on Miss Twilight's robes shimmered as she turned away to greet another student.

Twink's mother flew up, shaking her head. 'Teena's already checked herself in – I just caught up with her before she and Zuzu took off to Snowdrop Branch. The independent little beetle!'

Twink smiled. Yes, that was just like Teena!

Her mother's expression grew serious again as she drew Twink away from the crowds of arriving fairies. 'Now, Twink, promise me that you won't worry.'

Twink stared down at her pixie boots. How could she promise such a thing? Suddenly she remembered something, and she looked up. 'Mum . . . Gran went to school here too, didn't she?'

Her mother nodded. 'Yes, she did. And I'm sure she wouldn't want you to spend the summer fretting about her, Twink – she'd want you to have fun and enjoy yourself, just like you always do. All right?'

Twink took a deep breath. 'I'll try.'

'That's my girl.' Twink's mother gave her a warm hug. 'I'll send a butterfly as soon as there's any news about Gran. Have a good term, darling – and don't worry!'

Twink stood waving as her mother flew away. When she could no longer see her, Twink lowered her hand with a sigh. Not worry? How, when Gran had that awful-sounding illness?

Lost in thought, Twink picked up her oak-leaf bag and flitted towards the school. Suddenly a laughing voice called her name.

'Twink! Were you going in without me?'

Turning, Twink saw her best friend, Bimi Bluebell, come flying up. 'Oh! Bimi!' she gasped. She and Bimi always waited for each other on the first day of term, but this time Twink had completely forgotten.

The two fairies hugged tightly. 'It's so good to see you!' exclaimed Bimi.

'I know,' said Twink. 'It seems like ages!'

Bimi was easily the most beautiful fairy in the school, with her midnight-blue hair and silver and gold wings. But she was very down to earth, and hardly seemed to notice her looks. Now she narrowed her gaze, looking at Twink closely.

'What's wrong?' she asked.

'Nothing!' said Twink. She fluttered to one side as a stream of chattering second-year students flew past. 'I'm fine.'

'No, you're not,' said Bimi, following her. 'You look really pale.'

'I, um . . . caught a wing-chill over the hols, that's all,' said Twink quickly. The wing-chill made her think of Gran's illness, and she looked away. She hated lying, but she *couldn't* tell Bimi about it – or anyone else, for that matter. She knew she'd burst into loud, babyish tears if she tried.

'Come on,' Twink said, putting on a bright grin. 'Let's go up to Violet Branch and grab the same beds we had last term!'

'OK,' said Bimi doubtfully. 'But Twink, are you *sure* –'

'Race you!' broke in Twink. She zoomed through the doorway without replying.

Inside, Glitterwings Academy rose up like a tall, golden tower, with branch-corridors shooting off in all directions. Fairies darted in and out of these like birds, for as high as the eye could see.

With Bimi just behind her, Twink sped up the trunk, swooping around clusters of hovering students. Finally she landed on the Violet Branch ledge with a hop. The bright purple violets that hung over the doorway swayed in the sudden breeze from her wings.

'Phew! You won,' panted Bimi, touching down

beside her.

'It was close, though!' said Twink. She pushed open the door to their branch, feeling slightly better after the frenzied flight.

Violet Branch was just as she remembered: a crooked, sunny branch with different levels to it, and mossy beds tucked away in unexpected places. Violets hung over each bed like a sweet-smelling canopy.

A chorus of voices greeted them. 'Opposite!' shrieked one. A lavender-haired fairy hurled herself at Twink.

'Hi, Sooze!' said Twink, returning the hug. She and Sooze had been best friends once, and were still close – though Twink knew she had the best friend ever in Bimi now.

'Hi, Bimi,' added Sooze as they pulled apart. She fluttered her pink wings with a grin. 'We saved your old beds for you two, even though they're the best ones!'

'Thanks, Sooze – that's glimmery!' said Bimi. Though she and Sooze hadn't always got on in the past, they'd reached a truce of sorts these days. Twink was glad about it. Life had been very stressful when her two favourite fairies hadn't got on!

Twink and Bimi flew up to the smaller of the loft spaces. There were only two mossy beds up here, making a cosy little room of their own.

'Shall I take the bed by the wall again?' said Bimi. She took her cricket clock out of his cage, and fed him a bit of fresh leaf. He munched it happily.

'OK,' said Twink. She could see that Bimi was still concerned about her, and she hurriedly busied herself with unpacking. 'How were your hols?' she asked. 'Tell me everything!'

Bimi looked uncertain for a moment, and then shrugged. 'They were really good. We went to visit my cousins in Green Wood, and –'

Twink relaxed, smiling and nodding as her friend went on. Pulling out her favourite drawing of her family, she placed it on her bedside mushroom. Her parents and Teena smiled out at her.

I don't have a drawing of Gran, Twink realised with a pang. Why didn't she? Suddenly she thought she'd give anything to have a drawing of her gran, with her purple hair and wise smile. And she couldn't even write to Mum and Dad and ask them to send one, because they weren't at home.

'Twink?' said Bimi. Twink started guiltily. Her best friend stood with her hands on her hips. 'You haven't heard a word I've said, have you?' she demanded.

'No, I have!' said Twink. 'You were saying about – er . . .' she trailed off, trying to remember.

Bimi sighed. 'Oh, Twink. Let me know when you want to talk about whatever's bothering you.'

'Nothing's wrong, I *told* you,' muttered Twink. Why couldn't Bimi just let things drop? But she knew that Bimi was worried about her, which made her feel even more wretched than before.

Suddenly Twink spotted Pix coming into the branch. 'Hi, Pix,' she called out with the others.

Then an idea struck her. If anyone would know about the Doldrums, Pix would! Twink glided down to the main floor, landing beside the clever red-headed fairy. 'Did you have good hols?' she asked.

Pix nodded as she headed to the last empty bed. 'Yes, glimmery! I got loads of studying done. How about you?'

'Er – well, not *much* studying,' said Twink, taken aback. 'I mean, I only did what we were told.'

Pix shook her head as she started to unpack. 'We're in the Third Year now, Twink,' she chided. 'You can't afford to let yourself fall behind, you know.'

'I'm not *falling behind*,' protested Twink, stung. 'I

just didn't do any extra, that's all.'

From the look on Pix's face, it was clear that she thought it was the same thing! Twink glanced around the branch to make sure no one was listening. 'Pix, can I ask you something?' she said in a low voice.

'Of course,' said Pix, pulling a pile of schoolbooks out of her bag.

Twink drew a bit closer. 'I just wondered . . . have you ever heard of something called the Doldrums?'

Pix's eyebrows flew up. 'The *Doldrums*? Isn't it that awful condition fairies sometimes get, where they don't show any interest in anything?'

'I – I suppose,' said Twink.

Pix snatched up one of her books, flipping through it. 'Yes, I'm sure it is. Oh, it's dreadful! Fairies who have the Doldrums hardly even bother to eat, or laugh, or *anything*. Here, look.' Pix found the page she was looking for and pointed. Twink craned her neck, dreading what she might see.

'Wasps, it's even worse than I thought,' said Pix, frowning down at the page. 'It says that if a fairy has the Doldrums and something doesn't happen to snap them out of it, they might never be the same again! They just sit around feeling sad and gloomy for the rest of their lives.'

'How – how do you snap them out of it?' whispered Twink. Her wise, witty gran, sad and gloomy for ever? The thought turned Twink's blood to ice. No wonder her parents hadn't wanted her and Teena to know!

'*A shock of joy*, it says here,' read Pix. 'I suppose

that means they're surprised by something really nice, and it helps them get over it.' She shut the book, tossing it on her mossy bed. 'Why did you want to know?'

'I – nothing, it was just – just something I read in a petal mag,' stammered Twink, edging away. 'Thanks, Pix!'

To Twink's relief, no one seemed to notice that anything was troubling her – except Bimi, of course, watching from their loft. Usually Twink loved the way that she and Bimi could almost read each other's minds, but right now she thought she'd give anything for Bimi not to have a clue!

Sooze flitted over, nudging Twink with a friendly pink wing. 'Guess what?' she said.

'What?' asked Twink with a smile. At least she never had to worry that *Sooze* might read her mind – the lavender-haired fairy wasn't the sort to think too deeply about things.

Sooze lowered her voice. 'Well, I was just talking with Sili, and we reckon we know what Miss Twilight's big surprise is! We think that –'

'Hello, my lovelies!' boomed a voice. Mrs Hover, the matron, landed on the Violet Branch ledge and flitted heavily into the room. 'Are we all here now? Excellent! Time for the opening session in the Great Branch – come along now, flitter-flutter!'

Chapter Two

The Great Branch was the largest branch in the school, with gleaming wooden floors and rows of mossy tables. Every table had a flower hanging over it for each of the different branches, so that the Branch looked like a bright, sunlit garden – especially now, in summertime, when the days were so long and pleasant.

Twink flew to the Violet Branch table, perching on a spotted mushroom seat beside Bimi. Across the Branch, she caught sight of Teena sitting at the Snowdrop table, with her two friends Zuzu and Summer.

Teena grinned and waved at her, and Twink waved back. Thank goodness Teena didn't know about Gran! It would ruin her little sister's term.

Twink sighed. She wished that *she* didn't know either. If only she could turn back time, and not have overheard her parents' conversation! But Gran would still be ill regardless . . . and surely it was better to know than not know, wasn't it?

She started as Bimi nudged her. 'Good afternoon, Miss Shimmery,' chorused the school. Miss Shimmery, the HeadFairy, was hovering above the platform at the front of the Branch. Her rainbow wings glimmered in the sunlight.

'Welcome back, everyone,' she said warmly. 'I've just a few things . . .'

Pretending not to notice Bimi's worried gaze, Twink listened as the HeadFairy made her usual announcements: no high-speed flying in the trunk; uniforms required from tomorrow, *complete* with oak-leaf caps (the older years groaned at this); no bothering the water sprites in the school pond . . .

26

Twink gazed out of the window, wondering whether her mother had arrived at Gran's yet. How was her grandmother doing? Was the doctor still with her?

'Listen!' hissed Sooze from across the table. Looking up, Twink saw Miss Shimmery nod to Miss Twilight, who was smiling and looking very mysterious.

'And finally,' said Miss Shimmery with a twinkle in her eye, 'may I ask that all third-year students stay behind in the Branch after dinner, as Miss Twilight would like a word with you.'

An excited buzz rustled through the Third Year as Miss Shimmery drifted back down to the platform. 'Butterflies commence!' she announced.

The doors to the Branch swung open, and in flew the school butterflies, in a bobbing river of colour. Each butterfly carried an oak-leaf platter of food or an almond-shell pitcher of fresh dew, which they placed on the tables before fluttering off again.

'What do you suppose the surprise is?' asked Mariella, a pointy-faced fairy with silvery-green hair.

Mariella had been an awful pain for most of the time Twink had known her – though she finally seemed to have learned her lesson, and wasn't so bad now.

'Sooze and I have got it all worked out!' laughed Sili as she reached for a seed cake. 'We think –'

'No, let me tell it!' squealed Sooze, clamping a hand over Sili's mouth. Sili gave a muffled shriek, flapping her wings in mock struggle. 'A party!' cried Sooze. 'We think she's going to give us a super-glimmery party, and –'

'A party!' Mariella bounced on her mushroom seat. 'Oh, I hope you're right. That would be brilliant!'

Everyone echoed agreement. 'We haven't had any real fun in *ages*,' exclaimed a green-haired fairy called Ivy. 'It's been such hard work since we started Third Year!'

Twink tried to join in with the others while she ate, smiling and laughing. Secretly, though, she hoped Sooze was wrong. How could she possibly enjoy a party right now?

Finally the butterflies cleared away the tables, and the rest of the students departed. The Third Years remained behind, waiting expectantly.

Miss Twilight flew over to the third-year section and perched on the edge of a vacant table. 'Now then,' she said with a smile. 'I'm sure you're all wondering what the surprise is.'

Twink nodded along with everyone else.

'It's very simple,' said Miss Twilight. 'In my experience, third-year students often start to feel a bit fed up about now – the work is harder than you've been used to, there's a lot more of it, and suddenly it all seems very difficult. Am I right?'

Suddenly Twink's smile felt strained. She didn't want to think about things being difficult – they already felt much harder than she could handle.

'So,' continued Miss Twilight, 'I always make a point of arranging some sort of special activity for my Third Years in the summer term, just to ensure that they don't take themselves too seriously!'

Sooze and Sili nudged each other, their eyes shining.

'This year's activity . . .' Miss Twilight paused dramatically, 'is a treasure hunt!'

Despite herself, Twink almost laughed at the startled expression on Sooze's face. The rest of the Third Years were murmuring excitedly to each other, thrilled by the idea of a treasure hunt.

'I've hidden a series of ten clues around the school,' explained Miss Twilight. 'Each clue leads you on to the next, and the fairy who finds the most clues will win the grand prize!'

'When does the treasure hunt begin, Miss?' asked Pix eagerly.

Twink and Bimi exchanged a look. Pix would probably win, of course! The clever fairy always did better than anyone else at things like this.

'Tomorrow,' said Miss Twilight. 'You'll have three weeks to find all the clues – and I have to warn you, some of them are very tricky! Finally, on the last day, you'll have a day off from your lessons to complete the hunt.'

'Hurrah, a day off!' whispered Mariella.

'And does anyone know what that last day might

be?' continued Miss Twilight, looking around. 'It's a very important one.'

Ivy's twin sister Jade, who was in Carnation Branch, raised her hand. 'The solstice, Miss!'

The summer solstice – the longest day of the year – was a special time to fairies, who depended on the power of sunshine for so much of their magic.

Miss Twilight nodded, swinging her legs from the table as if she were no older than they were. 'That's right! So to round off the treasure hunt and celebrate the solstice, we're going to have a fairy disco on the star-gazing platform that night.'

'A disco!' hissed Sooze triumphantly. 'That's even *better* than a party!'

Miss Twilight's voice turned serious. 'Now, I'm sure I don't need to remind you that the treasure hunt is for your free time only, except on the final day. I still expect all of you to pay attention to your schoolwork over these next few weeks.'

She gave them all a stern look, and then suddenly smiled. 'But if I catch anyone paying *too* much attention to it, they'll have me to answer to!'

* * *

Back in Violet Branch, Twink got ready for bed, listening to the excited chatter that rang through the room. She made a face. Everyone was so keen to start the treasure hunt, but she just couldn't seem to care about it.

Slowly, Twink opened her jar of wing polish. Taking a pink rose petal, she stroked the polish on to her lavender wings, rubbing it in until they shone like jewels.

'The treasure hunt sounds like fun,' said Bimi. She brushed her long blue hair with a thistle comb, watching Twink carefully.

Twink nodded. 'Yes, it does.'

Bimi put down her comb. 'Twink, *won't* you tell me what's wrong? Please?'

Part of her wanted to tell Bimi, but the words just wouldn't come out. They were too awful, and too scary.

Twink gulped. 'I – I can't,' she muttered, looking away. 'I'm sorry, Bimi. I just can't.'

She knew Bimi must have seen she was close to

tears, though the blue-haired fairy didn't comment on it. 'All right,' said Bimi softly. 'But – but Twink, I'm sure that whatever it is, it's not as bad as you think!'

I wish that were true, thought Twink. But Pix's words echoed in her mind. Unless something happened to snap Gran out of the Doldrums, she could stay sad and gloomy for ever.

Down below, the other fairies were laughing and teasing each other about the treasure hunt. 'You'll win, of course, Pix!' called Kiki, a lilac-haired fairy with purple wings.

Ivy looked up from the petal pad in which she was always drawing. 'My sister Jade could win just as easily,' she said. 'She's very clever, you know!'

'Not as clever as Pix,' said Sili loyally.

Pix didn't say anything to this, but Twink noticed that she looked rather pleased as she changed into her nightclothes.

Ivy shrugged and added something to her sketch. 'Well, Jade was always the cleverest fairy at our old school. I don't think she was really trying last term;

we were both having too much fun swapping places.'

'Now, *that* was a brilliant prank,' grinned Sooze. 'I'd give anything to have done it myself!' The twins had only been at Glitterwings since the previous term, and for several weeks Ivy and Jade had had great fun switching uniforms and pretending to be each other during lessons.

'Imagine *you* a twin, Sooze,' said Mariella with an exaggerated shudder.

Sooze laughed and waggled her eyebrows. 'Who needs a twin?' she said. 'I've got an Opposite! Right, Twink?'

Up in her loft, Twink managed a smile. Sooze had called her 'Opposite' since their first term together, because Sooze's lavender hair and pink wings were the exact *opposite* of Twink's.

'Let's have a vote!' cried Sili. She leapt up on to her bed. 'Jade or Pix – who's going to win?'

'No!' burst out Pix, the tips of her pointed ears turning red. 'Stop it, you lot. Any one of us might win. It doesn't have to be me *or* Jade.'

Despite her protestations, though, Twink thought

that Pix sounded pretty confident. Of course she expected to win the treasure hunt – why shouldn't she? Pix had always been the cleverest fairy in their year, right from the very first term.

'What does it matter who wins?' put in Bimi, who had been listening along with Twink. 'The important thing is to have fun, isn't it?'

'Definitely!' said Sooze. 'And *I* certainly mean to. Especially at the fairy disco! Remember my dance from First Year, everyone?' She went into the wild, hip-wiggling dance she'd invented. The branch erupted into giggles.

The merriment lasted until it was time for glow-worms out. Lying under her petal duvet in the darkness, Twink stared out of the loft window at the stars. Now that no one could see, it was a relief to let a few tears escape down her cheek.

A beam of silvery moonlight shone through the window, resting on the drawing of Twink's family. Turning her head, Twink regarded it sadly. *Oh, I wish I had a drawing of Gran,* she thought again, wiping her eyes.

Suddenly a tingle of excitement swept over Twink's wings. Of course! Gran had been a student here at Glitterwings, and there was always a drawing made of each year group at the end of winter term. Each student was given a copy, but the school must keep copies, too. All she had to do was look in the library, and she'd see Gran!

I'll go in my free time tomorrow, Twink promised herself. She smiled up at the stars. All at once she felt better than she'd felt all day.

Chapter
Three

'Fog,' intoned Mrs Starbright. 'We fairies use it for many things. Who can tell me the most important one?' The Weather Magic teacher arranged her cobweb shawl about her shoulders as she waited for an answer. Twink shifted on her mushroom seat, glancing around her.

As usual, Pix's hand shot into the air. 'To cool down the earth,' she said promptly.

Mrs Starbright shook her head. 'That's one use of fog,' she said, 'but it's not the most important.'

'Oh!' said Pix in surprise. 'But I thought –'

'Yes, Jade?' interrupted Mrs Starbright. Ivy's twin sister was in a few of Twink's classes this term, and now she had her hand in the air, too, waving it eagerly.

'To give the sunshine a rest,' she said, tucking a strand of curly, light green hair behind her ear.

Twink found herself staring at Jade. She could never get over how alike Jade and Ivy looked! The only difference was that Ivy wore a violet petal dress with a yellow sash, like all the other girls in Violet Branch, and Jade was in the frilly pink Carnation Branch dress.

Mrs Starbright *tsk*ed. 'That's not the most important thing either,' she chided. 'My dears! The most important use of fog is *dramatic effect*!'

Sweeping her arms into the air, she closed her eyes and made a quick, complicated move with her wings. Grey mist began to form in the branch, rolling across the floor in great waves. Soon the fairies could hardly see each other.

'Yes, indeed!' came Mrs Starbright's voice from the front of the branch. 'What better way for us fairies to add a bit of . . . *atmosphere* to a place? Fog can soften rough edges, it can soothe, it can conceal! Now then, open your petal books to page –'

'Please, Miss, we can't see our books,' piped up Sooze. Twink grinned to herself as a snigger ran through the class.

'Er – yes,' said Mrs Starbright. 'Wait just a tick, while I get rid of the fog . . .'

Suddenly the grey clouds became so dense that Twink couldn't see her own hand. She gulped in alarm as the branch turned icy cold. It felt like the middle of winter!

'Miss, it's freezing!' complained Mariella's voice.

'Hang on . . . fog can be tricky sometimes . . . ah-ha! *There* we go.' Mrs Starbright sounded pleased with herself.

'Oh!' gasped Twink. Wet, chilly drops had begun to patter on to her wings and oak-leaf cap. Similar exclamations came from all around her. It was *raining*, right inside the branch!

Slowly, the fog disappeared. The fairies became visible again, though none of them looked very

happy. The class sat soddenly on their mushroom seats, wet and uncomfortable. The rain showed no sign of letting up.

'Remember, girls – rain is always an antidote to fog!' said Mrs Starbright. Her blue hair hung in damp strands around her face. 'Now then, open your petal books to page –'

'My book's too wet to read,' said Sili forlornly, holding it up. Its pages dripped on to the floor.

'Ah,' said Mrs Starbright, blinking. 'Yes, I suppose that's the one drawback to –'

The class sagged in relief as the magpie's call echoed through the tree, signalling the end of the lesson. 'Read Chapter Two!' called Mrs Starbright after them as they fled from the soggy branch. 'We do thunderstorms next!'

The class hovered outside the Weather Magic door for a moment, relishing the warm, dry air of the trunk. 'Thunderstorms!' exclaimed Bimi with a shiver. 'Do you suppose she'll conjure up one of *those* inside as well?'

Sooze wrung out her lavender hair. 'I hope not! I'd

like to learn how to *make* one, but I don't fancy being *in* one.'

'And anyway, I don't think dramatic effect *is* the most important thing about fog,' said Pix, flapping her wet wings crossly. 'That's not what our book says! I'm sure I was right.'

'I don't think so,' said Jade.

Twink gazed curiously at her. Was she really as clever as Ivy had said? She certainly seemed to be – though it was very strange to think that there might be a fairy in their year who knew more than Pix!

Pix's jaw dropped. 'Of *course* I'm right!' she exclaimed. 'It's very important to cool down the earth. If fog didn't do that, awful things could happen!'

Jade shrugged. 'That's true, but I did a special project on fog at my old school, and it's actually even *more* important to –'

Suddenly a group of fairies appeared, swooping close by. 'Hurry, you lot!' called Jax, a third-year student with spiky green hair. 'The first clue to the treasure hunt is up in our Common Branch!' She zoomed away up the tree.

The treasure hunt! They'd almost forgotten about it in all the excitement of the Weather Magic class. The fairies sped up the trunk after Jax. Pix and Jade led the way, each looking determined to get there first.

Only Twink and Bimi hung back. 'Aren't you coming?' asked Bimi.

Twink edged away. 'No, there's something I want to do in the library. You go ahead.'

'Oh,' said Bimi, looking worried. 'Well – why don't I come with you?'

Twink shook her head vehemently. 'No! It's nothing, Bimi. You go on – I'll catch you up later.'

Before Bimi could respond, Twink flitted away down the trunk. Glancing over her shoulder, she was relieved to see her friend spiralling slowly upwards towards the third-year Common Branch.

The Glitterwings library was a tall, lofty room with shelves reaching to its ceiling. Twink felt herself relax as she flew through its doors. There were no other Third Years in sight.

'Hello, Twink,' said Mrs Stamen warmly from her mushroom desk in the centre of the room. 'Can I help you with something?'

Twink fluttered across to her. 'I was wondering if there were drawings of old year groups that I could look at,' she said shyly.

'Yes, of course,' said Mrs Stamen. 'We keep the recent ones just over there.' She pointed to a low shelf beside a window seat in the corner.

'No, I mean *really* old ones,' said Twink. 'Decades old. Maybe even longer.' She felt her cheeks redden, and hoped Mrs Stamen wouldn't ask why she wanted to see such a thing.

But the librarian simply nodded. 'We keep those up in the Records section,' she said, indicating a shadowy corner near the ceiling. 'I'm afraid it might be a bit dusty, though,' she added. 'No one goes up there very much!'

'That's OK,' said Twink eagerly. 'Thanks, Mrs Stamen!'

The librarian hadn't been exaggerating, Twink found when she reached the shelves. It looked as if no fairy had touched these books in centuries! Their covers were coated with thick grey dust.

Brushing off one of the spines, Twink read *Glitterwings Academy Year Groups*, with a date under it. She frowned. Which year did she need?

Taking a guess, Twink opened one of the grimy volumes. Long-ago fairy faces stared out at her, with a list of names to the side of each drawing. Carefully flipping through the pages, Twink ran her finger down each list. Gran wasn't there.

Nor was she in the next volume, nor the next. Book after book showed no sign of Twink's grand-mother.

Maybe they didn't even do year drawings when Gran was a girl, thought Twink glumly, pulling out the last dusty tome. Opening the book, she glanced through the names – and then all at once she caught her breath.

There it was, beside the third-year drawing! *S. Flutterby!*

The drawing showed the Third Years flying in formation outside the tree. Gran was the fifth fairy in the second row, and Twink gazed down at the young girl in wonder. Gran had her arm linked through that of the fairy next to her. The two girls were pulling faces at the artist, laughing.

Why, Gran looked so young! And . . . and she seemed so happy. She had never even heard of the Doldrums back then, you could tell. Tears stung Twink's eyes.

'Twink?' whispered a voice.

Twink spun about in midair, clutching the book. 'Bimi! But I said –'

Her best friend hovered uncertainly beside her. 'Don't be cross with me, Twink! I had to come – I was too worried about you to bother with the treasure hunt. What are you doing?'

Twink wiped her eyes. 'Look,' she said gruffly, thrusting the book at Bimi. 'It's my gran. She's that one, right there.'

'*Really?*' breathed Bimi, staring down at the drawing. Bimi had met the older Mrs Flutterby on several occasions, and she smiled as she took in the girl's laughing features. 'But Twink, I don't understand –'

Bimi broke off as she looked up and saw the tears running down Twink's face. Hastily placing the book back on the shelf, she put her arm around Twink's shoulders. '*Please* tell me what's wrong,' she begged.

Somehow, Twink managed to get the awful story out. 'And sometimes fairies with the Doldrums never come out of them,' she finished wretchedly. 'They – they just stay sad and gloomy for ever, and –'

Sobs overcame Twink then, and she couldn't continue. Bimi put her arms around her. 'Don't cry, Twink! I'm sure it's not as bad as that. She'll be all right, she really will.'

'You don't know that,' sniffed Twink. But she felt better for having told Bimi, as though a weight had fallen from her. She managed a shaky smile. 'Anyway, that's – that's why I wanted to come to the library, to see if I could find a drawing of Gran.'

Picking up the book, Bimi opened it to the drawing again. 'Well, I'm glad you did. And Twink, she looks so much like you!'

'Do you think so?' asked Twink. The two girls stared down at the open page. Twink's heartbeat quickened as she saw that Bimi was right. She and Gran looked as if they could have been sisters.

The thought gave her a warm glow. Twink tucked the book under her arm. 'Come on, let's go and check this book out,' she said.

But as the two fairies turned to leave, Twink found her gaze drawn to the next shelf down. There were books there of all shapes and sizes – including one slim blue volume that was drawn out slightly from the others.

Twink's eyes widened abruptly. 'Bimi, wait!' she said, clutching her friend's arm. 'What's that?'

Chapter Four

Twink darted to the corner and pulled the narrow book from the shelf. Turning it over in her hands, she saw why her attention had been caught by it. Just visible through the dust, the cover had the word *'utterby'* written on it in a curling handwriting.

Twink licked her finger and wiped off the dust. The words sprang out at her. *This is the super-private journal of Silvia Flutterby. Keep out! This means YOU!!*

'Your gran's old journal!' cried Bimi, looking over her shoulder. 'But what's it doing *here*?'

'I – I don't know,' said Twink in a daze. 'The books on this shelf are all old schoolbooks and things like that – I suppose it just got mixed up with them, somehow.'

Her wings prickled as she stared down at the journal. Though she knew her explanation must be the right one, there was something very strange about finding Gran's journal just now – almost as if it had wanted to be found along with the drawing of Gran's year group.

But when Twink slid the two books across Mrs Stamen's mushroom desk, the librarian shook her head. 'I'm sorry, Twink, but volumes from the Records section can't be taken from the library.'

Twink felt herself turn pale. 'But this was my gran's!' she said. She showed Mrs Stamen the name on the little book.

The librarian's expression changed to one of wonder as she examined the journal. 'How interesting! Well, then, of course you have to take this, Twink. In fact, I'd say that it belongs to you and your family, rather than Glitterwings!'

'Oh, thank you!' cried Twink in relief. She slid the slim volume into her petal bag, fastening the clasp firmly.

'Now, what about the other book?' asked Mrs Stamen.

'This is Twink's gran, too,' said Bimi, flipping it open and pointing to the drawing.

'I see,' said Mrs Stamen. She tapped her chin thoughtfully as the two girls held their breath. 'Well, I can't let you take this book, Twink, but I

think we have extra drawings of the old year groups on file – shall I try and find a copy of it for you?'

'Yes, *please*!' said Twink. Hope tingled through her like fairy dust.

Mrs Stamen rummaged through the library's oaken filing cabinets. Soon Twink had not only a copy of the year group drawing, but one of Gran on her own, when she was just Twink's age.

'Thank you,' she whispered, staring down at it. 'Oh, Mrs Stamen, *thank* you!'

'Not at all,' laughed Mrs Stamen. 'That's what librarians are for!'

That evening Twink sat in the third-year Common Branch, trying to concentrate on her homework. She had decided to save the journal until that night, when everyone was asleep and she could read it in private . . . but the small blue book was unbearably tempting!

Finally Twink gave up and pushed her Flower Power project to one side. Glancing over her shoulder to make sure no one was watching, she carefully slid Gran's journal out from under her other books.

Super-private! shouted the words on the cover. Twink hesitated, biting her lip. *Should* she read the journal? After all, it did say *Keep out* – maybe her gran wouldn't want her to.

I'll keep it for her, and give it to Gran when I see her, decided Twink reluctantly. She started to push the journal aside . . . but somehow her fingers wouldn't let go of it. What if – what if her gran stayed in the Doldrums for ever? This little book might be all she had left of her.

I'll just take a tiny peek, thought Twink, her heart pounding. Quickly, before she could change her mind, she flipped to the first page.

It began:

A new term! It was so sparkly to see Aurora again, and good old Foxglove Branch. Aurora and I got beds next to each other, hurrah! She's brought a cricket clock from home. She says he's a real scamp, and he loves to play tricks. Once he hid Aurora's wing polish from her, only then he forgot where he'd put it and she didn't find it for ages! Anyway, we're having a brilliant time getting him to chirp songs for us. It's going to be such a sparkly term!

The study time went quickly as Twink read and read, forgetting all about her resolution to only take a peek. Gran had told Twink stories of her girlhood before, but nothing about her life here at school! Who would have guessed that her tall, elegant grandmother had got told off for whispering with her best friend during lessons, and that sometimes she'd broken the rules?

Twink grinned at another entry:

Jeni was saying yesterday that no one's ever been down in the school roots, and that there are monsters down there. Can you believe such nonsense, at our age? So Aurora and I sneaked down there last night, just to prove her wrong. Well, we didn't get eaten by monsters, but it IS pretty creepy – all dark and twisty, and it goes on for ages. At least we had Aurora's cricket with us –

he chirped songs so that we didn't get too scared. We almost got lost, but we found our way back finally and pretended to Jeni that we'd loved every second of it. Her face was a picture!

Twink stifled a giggle. Her gran had been even worse than Sooze!

A sudden commotion filled the Common Branch. Twink looked up, hastily closing the journal and hiding it under the rest of her books. Jax was standing on one of the fire rocks in the centre of the branch, loudly telling a story.

'Oh, you all should have seen it!' she laughed. 'Jade took one look at the clue, and *zoom*, she was off! Pix never even stood a chance.'

Jade and Ivy were sitting together as usual, studying at a mushroom desk. Jade shook her head. 'Honestly, Jax! It's not a contest between Pix and me, you know.'

Pix's cheeks were almost as red as her hair. 'No, it's not!' she snapped. 'And anyway, Jax, I *did* work the clue out – just not quite as quickly.'

'Well, I think you're *both* doing really well,' said Kiki mildly. 'I've got no idea what the first clue means!'

'Oh, you'll get it soon,' Jade assured her. 'Honestly, it's not hard at all, really.'

Pix seemed to grit her teeth at this. Tapping her yellow wings together, she scowled down at her petal pad.

Sooze flitted over and sat next to Twink. 'What do you want to bet she's working on the second clue right now, instead of doing her homework?' she whispered. 'You should have *seen* her when Jade worked it out first. I thought her wings were going to drop off from the shock!'

'What was the first clue?' Twink whispered back. Sooze unfolded a rose petal. In a low, dramatic voice, she read out:

'*Water, water everywhere*
That's where this clue is found
And if you were IN the water,
All around you would be round!'

Twink frowned. Did that mean the water was in a round shape, somehow? 'The school pond?' she guessed.

Sooze shook her head. 'That's what almost everyone thought. Loads of us went jetting down to the pond – Pix included. But nothing was there except the water sprites, and ooh, were they cross!' She put on a high-pitched voice. '*You bad fairies! Barging around looking for stupid clues and disturbing our nice, quiet pond – pah!*'

Twink laughed, imagining it.

Sooze lowered her voice. 'Do you know where the second clue turned out to be? The third-year Bath Branch! It's under one of the walnut-shell buckets, and –'

'Don't *tell* her,' chided Sili from the next desk. 'We're all supposed to work it out for ourselves!'

'That's all right,' said Twink quickly. 'I – I don't think I'm going to be playing.'

Sooze and Sili gaped at her. 'Why not?' demanded Sooze. 'It's the most glimmery thing that's happened in ages!'

Twink shrugged. 'I've got a lot to do, that's all.' Though it had been fun to hear Sooze's account, Twink couldn't imagine taking part in the treasure hunt herself – not with Gran so ill. It just seemed too silly to bother with.

'*Opposite!*' said Sooze, propping her hands on her hips. 'You *can't* –'

From across the branch, Pix suddenly banged her snail-trail pen down with a triumphant grin. 'Ha! I've got it!' Scooping up her petal pad, Pix flew from the room in a blur of red and yellow.

A startled silence fell, and then everyone burst out talking at once. 'The second clue! She's worked it out!'

Jax flitted to the doorway, peering out into the trunk. 'She's heading upwards!' she reported over her shoulder. 'Where do you suppose she's going?'

'Ooh, let's follow her!' cried Lola, Jax's best friend. Her thin face was flushed with excitement.

'No, we can't do that!' laughed Bimi. She was sitting near the window with a yellow-haired fairy

called Zena, explaining the Creature Kindness homework to her. 'We're not supposed to swap answers, remember?'

'Anyway, Jade, you must be getting worried now!' grinned Jax, coming back into the room.

Jade blinked. 'Why?'

'Because Pix is ahead of you!' cried Lola, bouncing on her toes.

Jade looked confused. 'No, she's not. I worked out the second clue this afternoon.'

'She's on the third one already,' boasted Ivy. 'That's my clever sis!'

The branch exploded into uproar. 'The *third* clue, and it's only the first day!' hooted Sooze, fluttering up into the air and doing a somersault. 'Oh, poor Pix! She'll never get over it!'

'When do you reckon you'll win the treasure hunt, Jade?' asked Jax eagerly. She perched on the edge of Jade's desk. 'Tomorrow? The next day?'

Shaking her head with a smile, Jade shoved Jax off her homework. 'You lot are awful. And *no*, I won't finish the treasure hunt by tomorrow, or even

next week, probably! The clues are getting much harder.'

'I bet she *does* win, though,' hissed Sili in Twink's ear. 'And I don't think Pix will like it very much!'

After glow-worms out that night, Twink waited until the only sound was that of soft breathing. When she was sure that everyone was asleep, she slipped Gran's journal out of her petal bag. She could hardly wait to read the rest of it!

Flitting silently up to the ceiling, Twink un-hooked one of the glow-worm lanterns and ducked back under her petal duvet. 'Glow-worm on – but only a little bit!' she whispered.

The plump green worm yawned. Slowly, a faint golden glow appeared. Twink snuggled down with the journal.

Time flew by as she read. Twink smiled as she turned another page. Gran had been just the sort of bright, bubbly fairy that everyone liked being around. Why, the two of them probably would have been friends, if they'd been the same age!

Then Twink came to the next entry in the journal, and her heart chilled:

I can't believe it. This is so awful that I can hardly even write it down. I've lost my ring! My special silver ring that I've had practically all my life. I thought it might be somewhere in the tuck shop, because I was helping Miss Nectar put some of the sweets away when I noticed it was missing – but it's not, I've looked everywhere!!

I feel so numb. I can't believe it's lost. Everyone's been helping me to search for it, but it's just GONE. I can't stop crying. That ring meant so much to me!

And to make matters worse, now Aurora's cricket is missing too. Poor Aurora! How can we both be so unlucky?

Oh, I'd give ANYTHING to have my ring back again!

Twink swallowed hard as she took in the tear-stained words. Oh, poor Gran! But surely she'd found her ring again, with everyone looking for it? Twink

flipped ahead in the journal, scanning through the entries.

Aurora's cricket had returned to Foxglove Branch the next day, much to Gran's best friend's delight. But Gran hadn't been so fortunate. Though she and her friends had searched Glitterwings for days, looking in every place they could think of, her ring was never found.

Slowly, Twink shut the book. She felt as forlorn as if it were her own ring that had been lost. *I wish I could find it for her*, she thought, tracing the letters on the journal's cover.

Suddenly Twink's eyes widened. She knew it was a mad idea – it had all happened so long ago – but what if she *could* find the lost ring, somehow? Would that be enough to snap Gran out of the Doldrums?

Twink's heart thudded so loudly that she was sure it would wake the other fairies. 'A shock of joy,' Pix had said. Well, finding Gran's ring would certainly be that. It had obviously meant the world to Gran; she'd be thrilled to have it back again after all this time!

How could she possibly find it, though? It sounded as if Gran and her friends had looked everywhere in the school! Twink bit her lip. Still, the ring had to be *somewhere*, didn't it – even after so many years? So maybe she could think of something that Gran hadn't.

'I have to try, anyway,' whispered Twink, tickling the glow-worm's belly. His light faded, leaving Twink alone in the darkness. 'That's all there is to it – I have to try!'

Chapter
Five

'What will you have?' asked Miss Honey impatiently. 'Candied nuts, sweet seeds? Come along, girl, there's a queue behind you!'

Hovering at the tuck shop counter, Twink glanced over her shoulder at the queue of first-year students. 'Well – I don't want to buy anything,' she confessed. 'I just wondered if you need any help.'

'*Help?*' Miss Honey stared at her in amazement. 'Why should I need help selling sweets to *you* lot?'

'You just . . . look really busy,' faltered Twink. She was certain that Miss Honey – a thin, bad-tempered fairy with drooping gold wings – would tell her to flap off if she started talking about decades-old lost rings. But she had to get into that tuck shop – it was where Gran had first noticed that her ring was missing!

'I *am* busy,' snapped Miss Honey. 'Which is why you need to move along, if you're not buying anything! Next!'

A First Year with purple hair sped up to the counter. 'I'll have –'

'No, wait!' burst out Twink, thinking fast. 'I mean – you look really busy, but – but it's also a project I'm doing! We're meant to help one of the teachers for a few hours, and see what life is like for them.'

Twink held her breath, praying that Miss Honey would believe her. Peering into the tuck shop she could see teetering wooden shelves and dark corners. Oh, there were *loads* of places a lost ring could be!

Miss Honey snorted. 'See what my life is like, eh? Which teacher thought *that* one up? All right, then – you can sort all the sweet seeds according to size, if you're so keen.'

She lifted the counter up, and Twink shot into the shop. 'Thank you!' she said fervently.

'No chit-chat,' retorted Miss Honey as she banged the counter closed again. 'My life's not about chit-chat; you can write *that* in your report! Now, there are the seeds.' She turned back to the queue. 'Next!'

Twink stared in dismay at the overflowing walnut-shell bucket of seeds. This would take ages! When would she get a chance to search? Slowly, she started sorting.

Half an hour later Twink's fingers were aching, but the seed level in the bucket hardly seemed any lower. Even worse, her free hour would soon be over, and the tuck shop manager showed no sign of leaving.

Miss Honey appeared beside her, glowering. 'Is that all you've sorted?' she scoffed. 'Huh! In my day, fairies knew how to work!'

All at once an idea came to Twink. She nodded, trying to look downcast. 'I'm sorry, Miss Honey,' she said. 'I suppose you could have done it much better.'

Miss Honey frowned. 'Well, of course I've had more practice,' she admitted. 'Work, work, work, that's all I ever do!' Grabbing a broom made of dried twigs, she attacked the floor with it, stirring up great clouds of dust.

'I know,' said Twink, holding back a cough. 'All the other girls chose a teacher for their project, but I wanted to see what life was like for *you*. You work so hard, and no one really appreciates you.'

'True,' sighed Miss Honey sadly. 'Minding this shop, year in, year out – sweet seeds and candied nuts! Bah!'

'In fact,' continued Twink, 'I bet you'd like to take a break for a change! Why don't you go to the teachers' branch right now, and have a cup of warm nectar?' She clapped her wings together anxiously as she waited for Miss Honey's response.

The tuck shop manager couldn't have looked more astonished if Twink had suggested she fly upside-down. 'The teachers' branch?' she gasped. 'Me?'

'Of course!' said Twink. 'I'll mind the shop.'

'Why . . .' Miss Honey hesitated, clearly tempted by the idea. Twink stood very still, not trusting herself to speak.

'I'll do it!' decided Miss Honey suddenly. Grabbing a battered daisy-petal hat from the wall, she plopped it on to her head. With her chin lifted high in the air, she sped from the shop.

'We're closed!' Twink announced to a startled second-year fairy who had just skimmed up to the counter. She banged the bark shutters together, hiding the shop from the rest of the school.

At last! But she had to hurry; she didn't have much time to search. In a frenzy, Twink looked in every place she could think of – behind boxes, in dusty corners, under the counter.

There was no ring anywhere.

Twink bit her lip. Where else could she check? The tuck shop was only small; there just weren't that many places a ring could be! She gazed glumly at the floor . . . and then suddenly she caught her breath.

Could the ring have dropped under the floor-boards somehow?

Twink's heartbeat quickened. *Of course!* That was one place Gran hadn't mentioned looking – and the tuck shop floor was made from old planks of wood, full of knotholes. A ring could easily tumble down one!

The bark shutters rattled. 'Knock, knock!' cried a merry voice.

Twink started. 'Miss – Miss Honey?' she gasped. She flew to undo the shutters and lifted open the counter.

The tuck shop manager swept back into the little room. 'Ooh, that was lovely!' she cooed, taking off her hat. 'I don't know why I've never gone before. They even gave me a slice of nectar cake!'

'That's great,' said Twink as the magpie's call signalled the end of her free hour. She rubbed her wings together. 'Er – I'm sorry that I shut the shop. I – um –'

Miss Honey waved this away with her hand. 'Not to worry, my dear! I expect you needed a break, too. There's a lot to be said for breaks! I plan to take plenty of them from now on.'

'Oh good,' said Twink weakly. Wasps! The rest of the school wouldn't thank her for that! Still, at least Miss Honey looked happy.

Twink flew from the shop to her next lesson. Maybe Miss Honey was in a better mood now, but Twink still didn't think she'd agree to tear up her shop's floorboards! How on earth was she going to check under them?

Swooping into the Fairy Dust branch, Twink stopped short, blinking in surprise. The room was completely empty, apart from Miss Sparkle standing at the front of it.

The teacher shook her head. 'This always happens at this time of year! Well, I'm glad I've got at least *one* student who still takes my class seriously, treasure hunt or no treasure hunt!'

As the magpie's call sounded again, the missing fairies all arrived in a rush, talking eagerly as they flurried into the room. Pix took a seat, her face pink-cheeked with excitement.

Sooze flitted close to Twink. 'Pix has done it!' she hissed. 'She's on the fourth clue now – ahead of Jade!'

'Not for long,' laughed Ivy, overhearing her. 'You wait and see – Jade's cleverer than anyone!' As usual when she was in a class without her twin, Ivy sat beside Kiki. The two artistic fairies got on very well, and spent a lot of time together.

Bimi took the mushroom seat next to Twink, tucking her bright silver and gold wings behind her back. 'Where were you?' she whispered. 'I looked everywhere!'

'I'll tell you later,' Twink muttered back.

At the front of the branch, Miss Sparkle clapped her hands together sharply. 'All right, that's enough! Petal pads out, please. You'll be taking notes today.'

Twink sighed. She enjoyed Miss Sparkle's lessons when they got to use fairy dust, but her lectures were often long and dull. She uncapped her favourite snail-trail pen as Miss Sparkle began to speak.

'Now then, you all know that you can use fairy dust to transform objects, but it has other purposes as well. You can use it to locate lost fairies, you can leave a trail with it, you –'

Twink didn't hear anything after 'locate lost fairies'. Her hand shot up in the air. 'Can you use fairy dust to find lost *things*?' she asked.

Miss Sparkle regarded her drily. 'What sort of things?'

Suddenly aware that everyone was watching her, Twink lifted her wings in a shrug. 'I don't know. Like . . . a lost piece of jewellery, maybe?'

'Misplaced your diamond tiara again, have you?' sniggered Mariella. Twink made a face at her as the class giggled.

Miss Sparkle shook her head. 'No, if an item like that is lost, then the fairy dust has nothing to work with. You see, you need to have something belonging to the missing fairy before the fairy dust can locate him or her – it's similar to when humans give a scent to a dog, to help them sniff something out. Now, as I was saying – '

'Is there *any* magic that can find a lost item, though?' Twink blurted out.

Miss Sparkle almost smiled. 'Have you lost something, Twink?'

'Not really,' mumbled Twink. 'I just wondered.'

'Well, unfortunately, the answer is no,' said Miss Sparkle. 'Magic is much easier to use on living beings than on things like jewellery. But I hope you find whatever it is,' she added kindly.

Twink's cheeks were blazing. She took notes automatically as Miss Sparkle continued with her lecture, hardly even noticing what she was writing.

When Miss Sparkle wasn't watching, Bimi slipped a scrap of petal across to Twink. *What have you lost? Can I help?* was written on it in Bimi's neat, curly handwriting.

Something of Gran's, Twink wrote in reply. *I'll show you in her journal later.*

Maybe Bimi *could* help somehow, thought Twink as she passed the note on to Bimi's mushroom desk. Her father always said that four wings were better then two when it came to solving a problem!

At the end of the lesson, Miss Sparkle took a sheaf of petal pages from her desk. 'I've marked the essays that you wrote over the holidays. You've done very well, most of you. One of my third-year students even got a hundred per cent.'

A few fairies turned to grin at Pix – but when Miss Sparkle handed their essays back, Pix stared down at hers with a dazed expression. Craning to see, Twink could just make out a large red *97* on Pix's petal.

'Miss Sparkle – was it Jade in your other class who got the hundred per cent?' asked Pix in a strangled voice.

Miss Sparkle turned to her in surprise. 'Pix, that's

none of your business. But yes, since you ask, it was. She's an excellent student.'

'Oh,' mumbled Pix. She shoved the petal away in her bag. When the magpie's call rang through the school, she was the first one from the branch, jetting away before anyone could speak to her.

Twink stared after her in surprise. How could Pix be so upset over only three points? She always did so well in school – and it wasn't as if she had anything else to worry about.

Unlike Twink. Her heart felt heavy as she slowly packed up her books. Her parents had been at Gran's for several days now, yet she hadn't heard anything from them. Gran must still be very poorly, lost in her Doldrums.

I've got *to find that ring*, Twink thought, slinging her petal bag over her shoulder. *I've just got to!*

Chapter Six

'Bimi, are you sure about this?' whispered Twink as the two friends spiralled down the shadowy trunk. Her best friend rarely broke the rules – and here she was sneaking out of Violet Branch with Twink after midnight!

'Yes, definitely,' said Bimi softly. 'Chirpy, be *quiet*,' she urged her cricket. He sat in his cage squeaking happily to himself, clearly thrilled to be out on an adventure.

'Here's the tuck shop,' said Twink, swooping to land on the dark ledge. 'Now, how do we get in?'

she wondered. The bark shutters over the counter were firmly locked.

Bimi's pretty face creased for a moment, and then she smiled. 'Easy! Watch.' Taking hold of the bottom of the shutters, she pulled them towards her until a small gap appeared underneath them. 'In you go, Chirpy,' she said, freeing the cricket. 'Open the shutters for us from the inside!'

The gleaming brown insect scooted easily through the hole, disappearing from view. Several seconds passed. Twink nibbled her thumb as she hovered. 'Do you think he understood?' she asked.

'Chirpy!' hissed Bimi, cupping her mouth with her hands against the shutters. 'Let us in, it's important!'

In answer there was a pattering noise, like several sweet seeds falling on to the floor. The distinct sound of munching floated out.

Bimi tapped her foot in the air. '*Chirpy* –' she started. With a faint *click*, the shutters suddenly swung open.

The two fairies shot inside. Hastily, Twink closed the shutters again. 'Glow-worm on!' she said.

The tuck shop came into view. Chirpy blinked at them from the floor, surrounded by crumbs. 'You bad thing!' scolded Bimi lovingly, picking him up and cuddling him.

'How do we do this?' wondered Twink, gazing down.

When Twink had shown Bimi her gran's journal and explained where she thought the ring might be, her best friend had had the idea of using Chirpy to find it for them – but there was still the problem of how to get him under the floorboards!

Walking slowly across the floor, Bimi paused as one of the boards squeaked. 'There!' she said. 'That one's loose! So if we just –'

Crouching down, Bimi inserted her fingers into one of the board's knotholes and tugged. It groaned in protest. Twink added her strength to Bimi's, pulling as hard as she could. *Pop!* All at once the board flew out, sending the two fairies flying.

'Brilliant!' cried Twink, staring into the dark hole. 'Look, it goes right under the floor!'

'Right, Chirpy, in you go,' said Bimi, scooping

him up. 'And if you find the ring, I'll buy you candied nuts for a year!'

Twink and Bimi listened tensely as the little insect crept about under the floor. Once or twice he paused, and Twink's pulse quickened – but he always continued.

Suddenly her ears perked up. 'Listen!' she breathed.

It sounded as if Chirpy were dragging something towards them. Twink stared at the hole, hardly daring to move. All at once the cricket's sleek brown head popped out. In his mouth he held a gold ring with a shiny blue stone.

'He found it!' shrieked Bimi. She clapped her hand over her mouth and glanced towards the closed shutters.

Twink's heart had leapt when she first saw the ring . . . but now she shook her head sadly. 'No, that's not it,' she said. 'Gran's ring was silver, she says so in her journal.' She took the ring from Chirpy and examined it. 'Besides, look – it's got initials inside it. *GH.*'

'Geena Honey!' realised Bimi. 'It's Miss Honey's ring – she must have lost it working in the shop.'

'Was that the only ring down there, Chirpy?' Twink asked the cricket.

He nodded morosely, and Bimi patted his dusty head. 'Never mind, you tried,' she soothed. 'You'll still get your candied nuts.'

'Well, that's that, I suppose,' said Twink as the two friends replaced the floorboard. She managed a smile, though she felt more like crying. 'And it seemed like such a good idea, too!'

'It *was* a good idea,' insisted Bimi. As they turned to leave, she laid the gold ring gently on the counter, so that Miss Honey would see it when she arrived the next morning. 'And we'll think of another one, Twink. We'll find your gran's ring somehow, I promise!'

But in the days that passed, this began to seem more and more impossible. Twink and Bimi looked everywhere in the school they could think of – the Great Branch, the library, all of Gran's old classrooms.

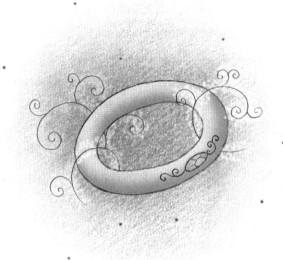

They even managed to search her old branch, with the help of some of the Foxglove fairies.

There was no ring anywhere.

'Oh, this is hopeless!' moaned Twink several weeks later, flopping on to her bed. 'Why did I ever think I could find it? It's been lost for *years*. It could be anywhere!' It was the half hour before glow-worms out, and the two girls were getting ready for bed.

Down below, the other Violet Branch fairies were

talking eagerly about the treasure hunt. The solstice was now the very next day, and Pix and Jade were wing and wing, with nine clues each. Only one clue remained to be found – but by which fairy?

'Pix, of course!' laughed Sooze, flipping back her lavender hair. 'But either way, tomorrow we get to dance the night away at our disco – I can hardly wait!' She wiggled and twirled down the length of the branch.

'*And* we get the day off, too,' said Mariella with great satisfaction.

'Anyway, are we having a vote, or not?' teased Ivy with a mischievous expression. 'Because Jade will win, you know, not Pix!'

Rolling over on to her stomach, Twink peered down to the main floor. Though she knew Ivy was only joking, Pix wasn't laughing. In fact, she looked rather quiet and tense.

I can't believe she's so worked up about a stupid contest! thought Twink. It seemed very unfair when Twink herself had such real things to worry about.

She had finally received a letter from her mum a

few days earlier, and it hadn't contained good news. Gran hadn't improved. The doctor was worried, and was talking about sending Gran to a special fairy hospital many miles away.

After receiving this letter, Twink had crept away to the old caretaker's stump behind the school to have a good cry. She had told only Bimi about its contents. Thank goodness the other fairies were too involved with the treasure hunt to notice anything was wrong!

It's hopeless, Twink thought again, struggling against tears. *I wanted so much to help Gran . . . but I can't do anything after all.*

Bimi had been combing her long blue hair in thoughtful silence. 'I don't know, Twink,' she said suddenly. 'I've been thinking . . . it really is very odd that you found your gran's journal, isn't it?'

Twink nodded, remembering the wing-tingling moment when she'd first spotted it. 'Yes, but I don't see what that has to do with it.'

Bimi put her comb down. 'Well, maybe – maybe the ring has some sort of magic to it, and it *wants* to be found. I don't see why else you would have discovered that journal, just when you were looking for drawings of your gran! It's too strange.'

Twink sat up, turning the idea over in her mind. 'Maybe,' she said slowly. 'Or maybe it's just a coincidence.'

Bimi pulled a face. 'Coincidence is what humans say when they don't understand magic! No, I reckon you came across that journal for a reason: to help you find your gran's ring, because it might get her out of the Doldrums.'

Twink stared at her. 'But Bimi – if that's true, then the answer to where the ring is *has* to be in the journal somewhere!' she cried. 'The ring wouldn't have bothered leading us to it otherwise.'

Bimi nodded. Quickly bouncing on to Twink's bed, she grabbed the journal up from Twink's bedside mushroom. 'Come on, let's look through it now – we must have missed something!'

But no sooner had they opened the journal than there came a screech from below. '*Bimi!*' called Sili. 'Your stupid cricket's got under the floorboards *again* – I can hear him scuttling around down there!'

A quick glance at Chirpy's empty cage showed that Sili was right. With a groan, Bimi flitted down to the main floor.

Twink followed, rolling her eyes. Chirpy was becoming very tiresome with his new hobby! Ever since they'd returned from the tuck shop, Bimi's cricket had crept off at every opportunity to explore under the floorboards of Violet Branch.

Bimi crouched in the corner, where the floor didn't quite meet the uneven wall of the tree. 'Chirpy!' she called into the hole. 'Chirpy, come out of there!'

Pix shook her head. 'Crickets *love* dark places,' she said. 'Once they get a taste for them, they always want to return. And you know how forgetful crickets are. Sometimes they even forget the way out again!'

'Well, he'd better not forget the way out while he's crawling about under my bed,' said Sili crossly, tightening the belt of her dandelion-fluff dressing gown. 'He kept me awake for hours last night!'

Twink stood very still as several ideas crashed together in her head. Crickets loved dark places, and always wanted to return to them. Gran and Aurora had taken Aurora's cricket with them when they sneaked down into the roots. And Aurora's cricket had been a trickster, who liked to hide things . . . *and then forgot where he had put them*!

'Ha! Got you!' said Bimi, dragging Chirpy from the hole. The cricket chirped in protest, kicking his long dark legs.

'Bimi, listen!' hissed Twink once they were back in their loft. Quickly, she shared the thoughts that had occurred to her.

'So maybe Aurora's cricket took your gran's ring for a prank,' said Bimi slowly, latching Chirpy back into his cage. 'And he went back to the roots with it, because he liked it down there.'

'Yes!' cried Twink. She snatched up the journal, leafing hurriedly through its pages. 'Because look at this – Aurora's cricket went *missing* around the same time Gran noticed her ring was gone! He came back the next day, but everyone was so upset that they didn't make the connection. Bimi, I bet you anything that he took the ring down there and then forgot about it!'

Bimi nodded eagerly. 'It all makes sense. Your gran first *noticed* she'd lost the ring in the tuck shop, but that doesn't mean it's actually where she lost it! It could have been gone for hours already, couldn't it?'

On Twink's mushroom table, the drawing of Gran – which Twink had framed with some pretty, polished twigs – seemed to smile at them. Twink grinned back at it. They were right – she just *knew* it!

'We've got to go down there,' she said, shutting the journal with a snap. 'It's brilliant that we've got the day off tomorrow – we can go really early, and –'

She stopped. Bimi had suddenly sunk on to her bed, looking almost green. 'Twink, I – I can't,' she whispered.

'You won't help me? But . . .' Twink trailed off, a hard lump filling her throat.

'Oh, Twink, you know I would if I could!' wailed Bimi softly. 'But I can't stand small, dark places. They make my wings go all clammy, and – and I get dizzy so that I can barely breathe . . .' she shuddered wretchedly.

Instantly contrite, Twink sat beside Bimi and put her arm around her. 'Never mind,' she said. 'I'll be fine alone, Bimi, honestly I will. And I couldn't have made it this far without your help!'

'Are you sure?' asked Bimi, wiping her eyes.

Twink nodded firmly. 'Of course. Now that we know where the ring actually is, it'll be ant's play to find it!' But deep down, she wasn't nearly as confident as she sounded. Gran had said that the roots went on for ages . . . and a ring was such a small thing to be searching for.

Bimi looked as if she were thinking the same thing. 'Could someone else go with you?' she asked anxiously. 'Maybe – maybe Sooze, or –'

'Pix!' burst out both fairies at once. Twink grinned in relief. Oh, of course! The clever fairy would have all sorts of ideas about where to find the ring. With Pix helping, she'd find it in no time!

'I'll ask her after breakfast tomorrow,' said Twink. She squeezed her best friend's hand tightly. 'Oh, Bimi – I think I might really be able to help Gran now!'

Chapter Seven

'Are you mad?' demanded Pix.

Twink blinked. 'No, I – I just thought –' The two fairies were hovering outside the Great Branch after breakfast, as the rest of the school flew past them in a bright, fluttering stream.

'Of course I can't go with you *now*,' cried Pix. 'It's the final day of the treasure hunt! Jade's already searching – I've got to get going!'

Twink gaped at her. 'But Pix, this is to help my gran! Don't you understand? There's no time to lose; she'll have to go to a special fairy hospital if something doesn't happen to cheer her up –'

'Yes, but – but can't we go tomorrow?' said Pix, looking distressed. 'Or just after the treasure hunt is over? I don't mind missing the disco –'

'*No!*' shouted Twink. Her fists clenched. 'I have to go *now*, Pix – I can't wait for your stupid treasure hunt. I can't believe *that's* more important to you than helping my grandmother!'

'But Twink, I've *got* to beat Jade, I've just got to!' burst out Pix. 'You don't understand.'

The trunk seemed very quiet as Twink hung in the air, staring at the fairy she had thought was her friend. 'You're right, Pix,' she said coldly. 'I don't understand at all.'

Without waiting for a reply, she sped off down the trunk as fast as she could.

The small door sat half hidden in the shadows at the bottom of the trunk. Twink landed in front of it, her heart beating hard. Bimi wasn't the only one who didn't like dark, enclosed places – most fairies hated the idea of being underground. And aside from that, the roots were strictly off-limits to students.

But Twink had no choice. It was for her gran. Looking over her shoulder to make sure no teachers were watching, she took a deep breath and pushed open the door.

It was darker than the blackest night imaginable. 'Er – glow-worms on?' Twink squeaked. To her great relief, a few lanterns hanging from the ceiling came to life, showing a tunnel leading downwards.

Taking a deep breath, Twink stepped in and shut the door behind her.

The tunnel plunged into the ground just as Gran had described, twisting and turning. The roots were obviously used as a storage area – there were wooden doors to either side, with signs saying things like *Saddles for Birds (All Sizes)* and *Spare Sparkle Marks.*

Unhooking one of the lanterns from the ceiling, Twink peered into every nook and knothole she passed, praying that Gran's ring would appear. Then she stopped abruptly. In front of her, the tunnel split off into three directions.

Twink tapped her wings together. Which way would Aurora's cricket have chosen?

Hesitantly, she entered the right-hand tunnel. But she had hardly taken a few steps when this one branched into two directions as well. Twink chose left this time, and trudged onwards with a sinking heart.

There must be *hundreds* of roots! She couldn't explore them all. It was even worse than that

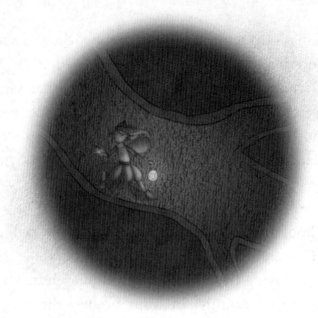

expression humans used – finding a needle in a haystack. That was nothing compared to finding a ring in the roots!

Twink walked for what seemed like ages, choosing roots randomly. All the while, she was heading deeper and deeper underground . . . and she still had no idea where her gran's ring was.

Suddenly a terrible thought struck Twink. She had no idea where *she* was either. All those different directions she'd taken, and now she didn't remember which ones! Trying not to panic, Twink hastily began to retrace her steps. Oh, why hadn't she brought a piece of chalk to mark her way? What a moss brain she'd been!

Rounding a corner, Twink stopped short, her eyes widening. A glittering pink and gold light was heading straight towards her.

Twink stared as the small globe of fairy dust flew right up to her and stopped, bobbing up and down as if pleased to see her. A sparkling trail hung in the air behind it.

'Twink!' called a familiar voice. 'Twink, where are you?'

'Pix, I'm here!' shouted Twink, her wings drooping with relief.

Pix appeared around the curve of the root. 'The spell worked!' she said, looking pleased. She was carrying a large bundle with a petal cloth draped over it.

'What spell?' asked Twink.

Pix flitted up next to her. Putting down whatever she was carrying, she cupped the fairy dust globe in her hands. Immediately, the trail vanished into it with a dramatic, sparkling swirl.

'The missing fairy spell,' said Pix, slipping the fairy dust into a little pouch on her hip. 'Don't you remember? Miss Sparkle explained about it in class. I read ahead in our book to find out how to do it.'

'Oh, well done!' breathed Twink. Then she remembered how cross she had been with Pix, and her eyebrows creased. 'But – what are you doing down here, anyway? I thought –'

Even in the dim light from the lantern, Twink could see Pix's cheeks turn red. 'Oh, Twink, I'm sorry! I was being a total wasp brain. Will you forgive me?'

Twink frowned in confusion. 'Well, of course I will – but what about the treasure hunt?'

Pix shrugged. 'Jade will win it, I suppose,' she said shortly. 'But I'm here to help, Twink, and we're not leaving until we find your gran's ring.'

'Aren't we still lost, though?' said Twink anxiously. 'I mean, you found *me*, but – do you know the way out?'

'Of course!' grinned Pix. 'There's that other handy spell Miss Sparkle told us about – using fairy dust to leave a trail!' She pointed at a faint, sparkling line on the ground that Twink hadn't noticed, leading back up the tunnel. Twink and Pix smiled at each other.

'Come on,' said Pix. 'We need to go back to the start, and begin again from there.'

'Go *back*?' protested Twink. 'But . . . it's so far!'

'Yes, but we have to do this logically,' said Pix. She held up the bundle she'd been carrying. 'I don't know if this will work or not, but I think it's our best hope.' She pulled off the petal covering.

Twink stared. Pix had brought Chirpy along in his cage! The cricket blinked up at her.

'You see, crickets are all very similar in some ways,' explained Pix as they headed back up the tunnels. 'If Aurora's cricket took your gran's ring and hid it down here, then he probably put it in a place that he liked. So if we let Chirpy out at the start of the tunnels, then *he* might go to that same place – and all we have to do is follow him.'

'Oh, that's brilliant!' exclaimed Twink. Why

hadn't *she* thought of that? She gave an excited skip. 'Pix, I don't know why you're so bothered about Jade winning the treasure hunt – everyone knows how clever you are!'

Pix winced. For a moment, the only sound was the tread of their pixie boots on the rough bark floor. Finally the red-haired fairy sighed.

'Twink, I know I've been such an idiot . . . but I felt like I just *had* to win. I – I couldn't bear the thought of not being the cleverest any more.' She made a face. 'I'm sorry, I don't mean to sound stuck-up about it –'

'You don't sound stuck-up at all,' said Twink, surprised. 'You *are* the cleverest. You get the highest marks of anyone.'

'Not any more,' said Pix glumly. She kicked at the floor. 'Twink, I don't think anyone knows how hard I have to work to get such good marks. But Jade doesn't even seem to try, and she *still* does better than me. She's . . . she's just cleverer, that's all.' Pix sounded close to tears.

Twink gazed at her friend in mingled sympathy and confusion. 'Maybe she is, but . . . well, Pix, what does it matter? You still do better than almost anyone.'

'Oh, but that's not good enough!' burst out Pix. 'You don't understand. My parents are always so excited when I come out top of the class; they brag about it to all their friends. And – and more than that . . .' she trailed off.

'What?' pressed Twink.

Pix took a deep breath. 'Well – if I'm not the cleverest fairy, then what *am* I? I've always been the cleverest, and everyone knew it! Now I'm not any more – Jade is. So . . . where does that leave *me*?'

Guilt pinched Twink. She had assumed that Pix's problems weren't as important as her own, but Pix had clearly been going through an awful time as well. She tucked her arm through Pix's and squeezed it hard.

'You're *Pix*,' she said warmly. 'You're clever, and funny, and you're a wonderful friend. You don't always have to be the best – we all like you anyway, just for yourself.'

Pix wiped her eyes. 'Thanks,' she mumbled, trying to smile. 'I suppose you're right. Anyway, look – here we are, back at the entrance!'

Sensing that Pix didn't want to talk about it any more, Twink knelt on the floor beside her as Pix opened Chirpy's cage. 'There you are, Chirpy,' said Pix, giving him a soft nudge. 'Just go wherever you

like, and we'll follow you!'

The cricket gave a joyful chirp and sprang away down the tunnel, with the two fairies racing after him. The fairy dust trail twinkled behind them, showing the way back.

Chirpy chose his way without hesitation, heading further and further down into the roots. Finally he stopped in a small nook that nestled cosily against the wall. With a happy sigh, he settled down, curling his antennae over his head.

'This must be it!' breathed Twink. Holding up the lantern, she looked all around the little hole, moving Chirpy gently aside to check under him as well.

There was no ring.

'But – I don't understand,' said Pix blankly. 'He came here so quickly, like he knew exactly where he was going! The ring *has* to be here.'

'Wait!' gasped Twink. 'Pix, don't you remember from Flower Power? Root systems *grow* – they change all the time! The ring probably *is* here – but a piece of root may have grown over it.'

Holding up the lantern again, Twink checked the wall instead of the ground, inspecting it carefully. Sure enough, there was a bit of new growth curving over one section. In between the new growth and the old a long, narrow hole had been formed.

And from deep within it came a flash of silver.

'It's there!' yelled Twink, almost dropping the lantern. 'It's really there!'

'Chirpy, can you get it out?' urged Pix. 'It's too far back for us to reach!'

With an answering chirp, the cricket squirmed into the hole. A moment later he was out again . . . with a silver ring held triumphantly in his mouth.

'Oh,' whispered Twink. She gently took the ring from him. It was made up of three strands of silver plaited together in a delicate band, with a single green stone that winked up at her.

'Pix, we've found it!' she choked out. 'We've really found it!'

'Hurrah!' shouted Pix. The two fairies hugged, jumping up and down. Chirpy nudged at their legs, and Pix laughed and scooped him into the hug as well.

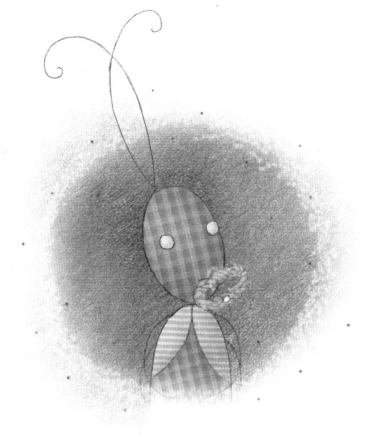

'And it was all because of you, you clever cricket!'

'Come on,' said Twink, putting the ring on her own finger for safe keeping. 'We have to go and see Miss Shimmery straight away – I've got to get this ring to my gran!'

Chapter Eight

Twink and Pix hurried back up through the tunnels. Before they had gone far, a sparkling pink and gold ball whizzed down the passageway towards them. As before, it stopped just in front of their faces.

'Twink, *there* you are!' cried a voice. A fairy with light green curly hair came racing up. Twink stared as she recognised Jade – and there were Ivy and Sooze, right behind her!

'Jade! What are *you* doing here?' asked Pix, looking stunned.

Jade caught up the fairy dust ball, tucking it away

in her pocket. 'Bimi told us what's going on,' she said earnestly. 'We want to help find your gran's ring.'

Ivy nodded. 'She hopes you won't be angry with her for telling, Twink – but she was getting really worried because you've been down here for so long.'

'Oh, *thank* you,' said Twink, overcome with gratitude. She had the most wonderful friends in the world! 'But look – we've already found it!' Grinning widely, she held up her hand, with the ring sparkling on her finger.

'Hurrah!' cried Sooze, flinging her arms around her. 'Opposite, that's brilliant!'

The fairies started back towards the trunk, chattering eagerly. Behind her, Twink heard Pix and Jade talking. 'What about the treasure hunt, then?' asked Pix. 'Did you win?'

Jade laughed. 'No, I left it the moment Bimi told me. I don't know who's going to win it now – it's almost time for dinner, and then it's the disco. But Pix, *how* did you and Twink find the ring?'

'It was mostly Pix,' put in Twink, hanging back

for a moment to join them. 'Oh, Jade, she was brilliant!' The fairies continued upwards, listening in admiration as Twink told the tale.

'I would *never* have thought of that,' declared Jade, fluttering her green and white wings. 'Pix, that was so clever of you!'

Pix looked sheepish. 'Well . . . I thought it was pretty glimmery the way you solved the fifth clue of the treasure hunt so quickly, too,' she admitted. 'It took me ages to work out that the *tree* was actually that drawing of Queen Mab's family tree on the wall of the Great Branch!'

'Oh, but what about the way you worked out Clue Seven?' countered Jade. 'I couldn't believe it! It took you *no* time at all, and –'

They had reached the entrance again. Twink hugged her friends tightly. 'I've got to go and see Miss Shimmery now,' she said. 'Thank you for your help, all of you!'

As Twink sped away up the tree she could still hear Jade and Pix talking, and she smiled to herself. Maybe Pix hadn't won the treasure hunt . . . but it

seemed as if she might have found something even better.

'I can't believe it,' said Miss Shimmery softly, turning the gleaming silver band over in her hands. 'Silvia's ring, after all these years . . .'

Sitting in Miss Shimmery's office, Twink shifted on her seat in confusion. The HeadFairy had looked more and more taken aback as Twink had told her about Gran's illness, and finding the journal . . . and now, examining the ring, she looked as if she were seeing a ghost.

Miss Shimmery caught Twink's expression and smiled faintly. Returning the ring to Twink, she folded her gleaming rainbow wings behind her back. 'My dear child, *I* am Aurora,' she said. 'Your grandmother and I were very close friends when we were both students at school here.'

'*You're* Aurora?' exclaimed Twink. Her thoughts spun wildly. 'But – but what about all the pranks that you and Gran played, and – and the trouble you got into in your lessons, and – *going down into the roots*!'

Miss Shimmery chuckled at her amazement. 'Neither of us was perfect, it's true. We were both high-spirited girls – though I might venture to say that it was normally your grandmother who thought up all the trouble we got into!'

'Oh,' murmured Twink in a daze. It seemed unbelievable that serene, white-haired Miss Shimmery had once been a young girl at Glitterwings, getting into mischief. And that she had then grown up to be the HeadFairy!

Miss Shimmery's expression turned serious again. 'You were wrong to go down into the roots without telling a teacher, Twink – but I understand why you did it. You won't be punished.'

She rose from her mushroom desk. 'And now I'll summon a hawk for us. We must hurry, and get this ring to Silvia straight away.'

'Gran?' whispered Twink. Her grandmother sat in a chair by the window, gazing listlessly out at the summer evening. She gave no sign that she had heard.

Twink knelt beside her. 'Gran, it's me – Twink!' She touched her grandmother's hand.

The hawk had flown them to her grandmother's house in record speed. Barely an hour had passed since Twink had sat in Miss Shimmery's office explaining matters.

But now her gran didn't even seem to hear her.

In the doorway, Twink's parents stood with Miss Shimmery and the doctor. Twink's dad had his arm around her mum as they all watched anxiously.

Twink swallowed hard and tried again. 'Look, Gran – I've brought you something,' she said. Slipping the ring from her finger, she placed it on her grandmother's lap.

At first Gran didn't seem to notice. Then, with a weary sigh, she looked downwards. Her expression didn't change.

'Don't – don't you recognise it?' faltered Twink.

'It's your old ring, that you lost when you were a student at Glitterwings! You were so upset at the time . . . Oh, Gran, don't you remember?' she pleaded.

'My . . . ring,' murmured Gran, gazing down at it.

'Yes, your ring!' said Twink's father, fluttering over next to her. 'Mum, you've told me about it before, remember? And now Twink's found it for you!' His hand squeezed Twink's shoulder.

'My *ring*,' Gran repeated more strongly. A faint light appeared in her purple eyes. Slowly – so slowly that Twink thought she was only imagining it at first – Gran began to smile.

Holding the ring up to the light, she turned it this way and that. 'I never thought I'd see it again,' she said. 'My old ring!'

Twink held her breath as her grandmother's smile grew and grew, until all at once joy was bursting across her face like a sunrise. She laughed in delight, slipping the ring on to her finger and holding it up to admire it.

'Gran?' said Twink softly.

Gran looked up. Her eyes widened, and she stared around her as if she had only just seen everyone. 'My darlings, what are you all doing here?' she cried. 'Alix, Jasmine – and *Twink*! Why on earth aren't you at school, young lady?'

'Mum, you're back!' burst out Twink's father. He hugged his mother tightly.

Gran shook her head as she patted his shoulder. '*Back?* And where am I supposed to have been, pray tell?'

'Hello, Silvia,' said Miss Shimmery warmly, coming forward. 'It's wonderful to see you again!'

As Gran exclaimed in surprised delight, Twink's mum flew to her side. 'Well done, darling,' she whispered in a voice choked with emotion. 'We tried everything, and nothing seemed to reach her. None of us knew what to do – but you did!'

'Yes, I can see that there's no more reason for me to stay,' put in the doctor, a short fairy with bright blue wings. 'And I must say I'm glad of it – she had me very worried!'

'Is Gran really all right now?' Twink asked

anxiously. She rubbed her hands against her violet petal skirt. 'She won't slip into the Doldrums again, will she?'

'No, she'll be fine,' smiled the doctor. 'She's finally had that shock of happiness that we've all been trying to give her – I guess we just weren't shocking enough!'

Later, when they had explained to Gran all that had happened, Gran called Twink over and put an arm around her. Smoothing back her grand-daughter's bright pink hair, she said, 'My dear, I don't remember – did my journal explain why this ring was so precious to me?'

Twink shook her head, relieved that Gran didn't seem to mind that she'd read it. 'You just said that it was your favourite.'

'Yes, because my own grandmother gave it to me when I was very young,' said Gran. She traced the ring's smooth silver lines with her finger. 'I loved her dearly, and it was all I had of her when she died. Losing it felt like losing her all over again.'

Impulsively, Twink kissed her gran's cheek. 'I'm so

glad that I found it for you, Gran,' she said.

Gran took the ring off her finger and pressed it firmly into Twink's hand. 'I'm giving it to you, my dear. It's a ring that should be passed down from grandmother to granddaughter.'

'But . . .' Twink struggled to speak. The ring gleamed in her palm. 'Gran, I *can't* –'

'Of course you can,' smiled Gran. 'You'll give it to your own granddaughter some day. And meanwhile . . . thank you, my dear. With all my heart.'

Slowly, Twink put the ring on her finger. It felt as if it belonged there. 'Thank you, Gran,' she said. 'I'll wear it always.'

Her parents and Miss Shimmery had stood silently through this, and now Miss Shimmery cleared her throat. 'Twink, we should be getting back to school,' she said gently. 'You'll still be able to attend most of the third-year disco, if we hurry.'

'Yes, all right,' said Twink happily. Now that she knew her gran was well again, the disco sounded brilliant!

Her parents beamed at her. 'Dance the night away, Twinkster,' said her father, ruffling her hair. 'You deserve it.'

As Twink and Miss Shimmery prepared to leave, Gran hugged Miss Shimmery with a laugh. 'And by the way, Aurora – I really might have known that that dreadful cricket of yours would turn out to be the culprit!'

The star-gazing platform had been transformed into a glittering wonderland of flashing crystals and different-coloured lights. A cricket band played loudly in one corner, and everywhere Twink looked, fairies were dancing.

Bimi rushed over to her. 'Pix told me the good news!' she cried, raising her voice to be heard over the music. 'Did you give the ring to your gran? Is she OK now?'

'Better than OK!' said Twink. Her heart felt as light as a floating feather. 'Oh, Bimi, wait till I tell you!'

'Your attention, please,' called Miss Twilight, hovering over the party. The music stopped as a hush fell over the platform. 'I am pleased to announce the winners of the treasure hunt. We have a tie, with nine clues found each! Would Pix Sunbeam and Jade Dewdrop please fly up and collect your prize.'

A tie! How absolutely perfect! Twink burst into applause with the rest of her year, clapping her wings as hard as she could. Pix and Jade smiled at each other as Miss Twilight handed them a large package, beautifully wrapped in golden dandelion petals.

'You'll have to share, I'm afraid,' said Miss Twilight. 'There was only one grand prize.'

'We don't mind sharing,' said Jade. 'Do we, Pix?'

Pix grinned at her new friend. 'No, we don't mind at all!'

There was more than one kind of prize to win, thought Twink as she watched the two fairies fly back to their places, holding the parcel between them and chattering eagerly. And she herself had won as well. Knowing that her gran was all right again was the best prize in the world!

The disco resumed, with the music even louder than before. Sooze started a fairy conga line, and Twink giggled as the fairies all linked together in a long, laughing chain, dancing around the platform to the music. 'Conga!' shouted Sooze at the front, waggling her hips.

As the summer moon rose high in the sky, it caught the green stone in Twink's ring, flashing brightly. Bimi had said that the ring had magic of its own, and she was right, thought Twink: it was the magic that existed between grandparents and their

grandchildren. That was why the ring had wanted to be found – not only to help Gran, but also to be passed along to Twink, so that she could give it to her own granddaughter some day.

Twink shook her head in amazement. Fancy *her* being old enough to have grandchildren! But she had only to think of her gran and Miss Shimmery to realise it was true. They had both been girls once, just like she was now. And one day she'd be their age . . . and maybe even as wise as they were.

But not just yet, Twink thought, dancing under the stars with her friends. Bimi grabbed her hands and they swung around in a circle, shrieking with laughter as the ring shone on Twink's finger. No, now was the time for her to be exactly what she was: a third-year student at Glitterwings Academy.

And it was the best thing in the world!

Turn over the page
and read the glimmery
beginning of Twink's
next adventure

From Friendship Dance

Twink Flutterby and her friends sat perched on mushroom seats in the Great Branch, waiting for Miss Shimmery, their HeadFairy, to address the school.

Twink smiled happily as she looked around her at the other fairies. A new autumn term! She had had a good summer holiday, but it was glimmery to be back at Glitterwings Academy. The oak tree school felt like home.

'I wonder what Miss Shimmery's announcement is going to be?' whispered Bimi Bluebell, her best friend. Both girls were sitting at the Violet Branch table. Other tables in the Great Branch had different flowers hanging over them, so that the large room looked like a bright, sunlit garden.

Twink shrugged. 'The usual, I suppose – uniforms from tomorrow, and no high-speed flying!'